Hiram's Red Shirt

By Mabel Watts
Illustrated by Aurelius Battagli

GOLDEN PRESS • NEW YORK
Western Publishing Company, Inc.,
Racine, Wisconsin

Copyright © 1981 by Western Publishing Company, Inc.
All rights reserved. Printed in the U.S.A. No part
of this book may be reproduced or copied in any form
without written permission from the publisher. GOLDEN®,
A LITTLE GOLDEN BOOK®, and GOLDEN PRESS®
are trademarks of Western Publishing Company, Inc.
Library of Congress Catalog Card Number: 80-85027
ISBN 0-307-02076-2/ISBN 0-307-60276-1 (lib. bdg.)
CDEFGHIJ

Hiram had a beautiful red shirt.
He wore it on weekdays and holidays.

He wore it when he painted the fences,

and when he rounded up the strays.

He wore it to picnics and to parties,

and when he twanged his guitar in the moonlight.
It was a good, sturdy, sensible shirt.

Every Monday and Thursday, Hiram washed his
shirt in the kitchen sink and hung it on the line to
dry. Then he carefully ironed out the wrinkles so it
would be ready to wear again the next day.

One morning Hiram was making pancakes for breakfast. Because he was feeling so fine and spry, he flipped one up tremendously high.

Suddenly he heard a *r-r-rip*. The beautiful red shirt had torn at the elbows!

But there was no time to fix it. Hiram had chores to do.

As soon as he finished breakfast, Hiram went out to the barn and milked the cows.

He fed the chickens.

He watered and brushed the horses.

As he worked, his elbows kept poking out of the holes in his sleeves.

"I'll have to patch my shirt," Hiram said to himself.

Hiram went to his room.
Snip, snip — off came the
shirt cuffs.
Stitch, stitch — in and
out went Hiram's needle.
"A little from here," he said,
"makes a little for there!"
The cuffs made excellent
patches for the elbows.

Hiram put his shirt back on and went out to feed the pigs. But without any cuffs, his sleeves flopped about and got in the way.

"I'll have to cut off my shirttails and use them to make new cuffs," Hiram decided.

Snip and stitch, snip and stitch. "A little from here," he said, "makes a little for there!"

In no time at all, Hiram had sewn fine new cuffs on his sleeves.

But now he had nothing left to tuck into his
jeans. His shirt flapped in the breeze, and he felt
chilly around the middle!

When Farmer Wills saw Hiram, he laughed.
"Looks like you've gotten yourself into quite a
pickle," he said.

"It wasn't very smart to use my shirttails to make new cuffs," Hiram admitted. "Now I suppose I'll have to cut off the bottoms of my jeans and use them to make a tuck-in piece for my shirt."

"Two wrongs don't make a right," Farmer Wills warned.

But Hiram didn't listen. Instead, he went back to his snipping and stitching. "A little from here," he said, "makes a little for there!"

Now the red shirt had new elbows, new cuffs, *and* new shirttails.

Hiram put his shirt back on and went out to feed potato peelings to the geese. Everything was fine until he walked into a patch of nettles near the goose pen. The nettles scratched and stung his bare legs.

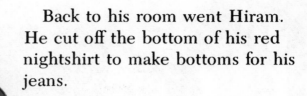

Back to his room went Hiram. He cut off the bottom of his red nightshirt to make bottoms for his jeans.

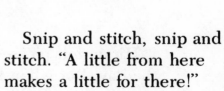

Snip and stitch, snip and stitch. "A little from here makes a little for there!"

Pretty soon Hiram had red flannel bottoms on his blue denim jeans.

Hiram felt pleased with himself for the rest of the day. But when he got into bed that night, wearing his cut-off nightshirt, his woolly blanket made him itch.

He tossed and turned and scratched all night. Poor Hiram didn't sleep a wink.

"A good breakfast will clear the cobwebs from
my brain," Hiram said the next morning. So he ate
a pancake, and thought. He ate six more pancakes,
and thought six times as hard.

"I made a lot of trouble for myself," he decided,
"when I took a little from here to make a little for
there. Now I'll have to take a little from there to
make a little for here!"

Snip and stitch, he took
the red flannel off his jeans
and sewed it back onto his
nightshirt.

Snip and stitch, he put
the blue denim bottoms
back onto his jeans.

Snip and stitch, the
shirttails went back to being
shirttails, and the cuffs
went back to being cuffs.

But now Hiram's elbows were poking out of his sleeves again. "This shirt has seen better days," he thought. "I guess there's only one thing left to do."

Instead of reaching for his scissors,
Hiram reached for his piggy bank.
And he went to the dry-goods store
to buy a brand-new shirt.

Hiram looked at pink shirts and purple shirts. He looked at plaid shirts and striped shirts. He looked at a beautiful flowered shirt that really took his fancy. But finally he decided to buy another red shirt, just like the old one.

When Hiram got home, Farmer Wills said, "You know, I could put your old shirt on the scarecrow out in my field."

"Nothing doing," Hiram replied. "This shirt is an old friend, and I don't want to part with it."

"Besides," he thought, "this old shirt will come in mighty handy someday, when I have to patch up my *new* red shirt!"